BETSY'S
LITTLE STAR

OTHER YEARLING BOOKS YOU WILL ENJOY:

BETSY'S LITTLE STAR

Written and illustrated by
CAROLYN HAYWOOD

A Yearling Book

Published by
Dell Publishing
a division of
Bantam Doubleday Dell Publishing Group, Inc.
666 Fifth Avenue
New York, New York 10103

ISBN: 0-440-40172-0

Reprinted by arrangement with William Morrow and
Company, Inc.

Printed in the United States of America

June 1989

10 9 8 7 6 5 4 3 2

CWO

To Mary R. S.
this book is lovingly dedicated

The author is grateful to
ELEANOR G. R. YOUNG
for composing the song that Star learned at
kindergarten and contributing it to this book.

CONTENTS

CHAPTER I

How Star Got a New Name

Star sat on the front step, holding Koala Bear. Koala was so old that most of his fur was rubbed off and his leather nose was peeled. It had turned from black to brown. He had lost one ear and this made him look lopsided. Even when he sat up straight he looked as though he were falling over.

Koala was a very old bear. He was older than Star and Star was four years old. He

1

really belonged to Star's sister, Betsy. Betsy was a great big girl of ten.

Koala had slept with Betsy every night until she was seven, and with Star every night since she had been a year old. It is no wonder his fur had been rubbed off and his nose was peeled and he had lost one ear.

Koala had always been such a cozy bear, and now Star had held him close almost all morning. She had needed something cozy, for she felt very lonely.

Today was the first day of school. Betsy had been up bright and early. She had run off to school before Star had finished drinking her orange juice.

Later, Lillybell called from the front gate, "Star! Star! I'm going to kindergarten. See! I'm going to kindergarten."

Star ran to the front door. There by the gate was Lillybell, the little girl who was one of Star's best friends. Lillybell had hold of her mother's hand. Lillybell was wearing a new dress, and she had a beautiful pink ribbon in her hair.

"Lillybell's going to kindergarten, Star," said Lillybell's mother. "It's too bad you can't go too."

Star watched Lillybell and her mother until they turned the corner. Then Star turned and looked the other way and she saw her friend, Rickie. Rickie was with his mother.

"Hi, Star!" he called out. "I'm going to kindergarten."

"Are you going to kindergarten, Star?" Rickie's mother asked.

Star shook her head. Then she saw Polly Lester and Rosemary Peters running up the street. They stopped at Star's gate and sang out, "We're going to kindergarten. We're going to kindergarten."

Polly and Rosemary were wearing clean white dresses, but Star was dressed in the overalls she had played in all summer.

Star's little underlip began to tremble and tears came into her eyes. She turned and ran into the house to her mother.

Mother picked her up and held her on her lap. Star put her head down on her mother's shoulder and sobbed. "Lillybell is going to kindergarten and Rickie is going to kindergarten. Everybody's going to kindergarten, 'cept me. I want to go to kindergarten."

"Hush, darling!" said Mother, rocking her little girl on her lap. "You'll go to kindergarten when you are five years old. Rickie and Rosemary and Lillybell are all five."

"I haven't anybody to play with me," said Star, rubbing her eyes with her fist. "Nobody at all. Even Thumpy is gone. He ran off after Betsy." Thumpy was Betsy's black cocker spaniel.

"Well, darling! You play with Koala Bear. Lillybell will be home from kindergarten at noon. You play with Koala Bear and wait for Lillybell."

So that was why Star had been sitting on the doorstep holding Koala Bear almost all morning. She couldn't think of anything to play, so she just held him very close.

Finally she decided to go for a walk. She called to her mother. "Mother, I'm going to take a walk with Koala."

"Very well, dear," Mother replied. "Don't go far."

"All right," said Star.

Star went out of the front gate and closed the gate behind her. She walked slowly until she reached the corner. Then she turned. She walked along until she reached the next corner. Then she turned again. Soon she was in front of Mrs. Jackson's house. It was right

behind her own house. Mrs. Jackson's garden was where Star and Lillybell and Betsy often played in the summer. Lillybell and her mother lived in the apartment over the Jacksons' garage. Lillybell's mother was the Jacksons' cook and everyone loved her and called her Clementine.

Star could hear Clementine singing in Mrs. Jackson's kitchen. Something smelled very good. It smelled like ginger cookies.

Star walked up the path that led to the kitchen door. When she reached the door, she said, "Has Lillybell come home from kindergarten yet?"

"My goodness, Star! No, indeed! Lillybell isn't home from kindergarten yet. Lillybell won't be home for over an hour," said Clementine, looking at the clock.

"I wish I could go to kindergarten," said Star.

"Well, now! You'll go when you're as big as Lillybell," said Clementine.

"But I want to go now," said Star.

"Here," said Clementine, "you take these ginger cookies and comfort yourself."

Star took the ginger cookies that Clementine handed her and said, "Thank you."

"Now you run along," said Clementine.

Star walked off, nibbling her ginger cookies. She walked down the path and up the street. She went around the block until she reached her own house. But she didn't turn in at her gate. She kept right on walking, for she had decided to walk to school and meet Lillybell. She had been to school with Betsy when Betsy had been in a Christmas play, and she had often driven in the car with Mother to get Betsy after school. Star was certain that she knew the way.

Star crossed the street and walked to the next corner. There she turned. She walked under a row of very big trees. She was sure that this was right. She remembered the big trees. After she had turned another corner she wasn't quite sure. She wondered where the car tracks were. But she could see a church in the next block. There was a church near Betsy's school. Star thought that she must be very near the school. Lillybell should be coming soon, for it seemed a long time since she had left Clementine. She had eaten both of her ginger cookies. It must be more than an hour!

She traveled on. She passed the church and

at the next corner she looked for the school. But there was no school in sight. Everything looked strange. Star didn't know where she was. Suddenly she knew that she was lost.

Just as the tears came into her eyes, Star heard a voice say, "Hello there, Twinkle, twinkle, little Star. I'll bet you're wondering where you are."

Star looked up and there was Mr. Tupper, the milkman.

"What are you doing here, all by yourself?" he asked.

"Everybody has gone to kindergarten 'cept me," said Star. "I was going to kindergarten to meet Lillybell."

"Well! You're away off," said Mr. Tupper. "But you come along with me. I'll get you back where you belong."

Mr. Tupper lifted Star up into the milk truck. Then he stepped in and they started off.

"I wish I could go to kindergarten," Star said to Mr. Tupper.

"Well, Twinkle! That's exactly where we *are* going. I have to deliver some milk to the kindergarten."

Star looked pleased. "Are you going to take the milk right inside?" she asked.

"Right inside," said Mr. Tupper. "And here we are!" he added, bringing the truck to a stop.

"It wasn't very far, was it?" said Star.

"Not at all," said Mr. Tupper. "But you have to know where you are, Twinkle."

Mr. Tupper stepped out of the truck. "Do you want to help deliver the milk?" he asked.

"Oh, yes!" said Star.

"Very well," said Mr. Tupper, as he lifted Star out of the truck. "Here's a bottle for you to carry. Don't drop it."

"I'll have to leave Koala on the seat."

"That's a good idea," said Mr. Tupper, taking Koala out of Star's hands. "Up you go, Koala! Mind the milk truck for us."

Mr. Tupper picked up a box. It was filled with bottles of milk. Star followed him, carrying her bottle of milk very carefully. They walked through a long hall. Finally Mr. Tupper kicked a door open and set the box on a long table. Little boys and girls were seated all around the table.

"Here's our milk!" they cried.

"I'm afraid I'm a couple of minutes late," said Mr. Tupper. "I have a new helper. This is Twinkle, Miss Morse," said Mr. Tupper to the kindergarten teacher.

"She's Star!" Lillybell called out.

"Well! Don't you know stars twinkle?" Mr. Tupper said.

All the children laughed and Rickie said, "Stars do twinkle."

"Can you wait while Twinkle drinks her milk with us, Mr. Tupper?" Miss Morse asked.

"I suppose so," said Mr. Tupper. "I'll drink some myself."

When the children had finished their milk, Mr. Tupper said, "Come along now, Twinkle. I have to take you home."

"Is Lillybell coming home soon?" Star asked Miss Morse.

"Very soon," Miss Morse replied. "You run along with Mr. Tupper. Lillybell will be home soon after you get there."

Star went out with Mr. Tupper. He lifted her into the truck and she took Koala Bear in her arms.

In a few minutes Star was back home. She thanked Mr. Tupper and ran in to her mother. "Mother!" she cried. "I've been to kindergarten!"

"Why, Star!" cried her mother. "What were you doing in kindergarten?"

"Drinking milk," said Star. "And I have a new name, Mother. I have a new name. They call me Twinkle."

CHAPTER II

How Star Learned a Little Song

The next morning when Betsy came down to breakfast, her mother said, "Betsy, you don't have to hurry this morning, because I'm driving you to school. I have to talk with Miss Preston about the parents' meeting." Miss Preston was principal of the school.

"Oh! That's great!" said Betsy.

"May I go too?" said Star, as she climbed up onto the telephone book that she always

15

sat on to make her high enough at the table.

"Yes, indeed!" her mother replied.

At a quarter to nine Mother drove out of the garage. Betsy and Star were beside her on the front seat.

"I'm making believe I'm going to kindergarten," said Star.

"Did you know that Star went to kindergarten with the milkman yesterday, Betsy?" said Mother.

Betsy laughed. "I heard about it," she said.

"And they call me Twinkle," said Star.

"Well, you do twinkle," said Betsy, hugging her little sister.

"Mr. Tupper thought of it," said Star.

When they reached the school, Betsy kissed her mother good-bye and jumped out of the car. "Good-bye, Twinkle," she said. "Don't get lost today."

"Bye," said Star, as she wriggled off the seat and jumped out of the car. "May I come with you, Mother?" she said. "So I can make believe I'm going to kindergarten?"

"Yes," said Mother, taking her by the hand. "Come along."

Star and Mother crossed the street and walked up the front steps of the school. Right inside the big front door there was a bench.

"Here, dear," said Mother, "you sit on this bench and wait for Mother. I won't be very long. You can watch the boys and girls come into school."

Star sat on the bench and swung her legs. She could hear the children shouting in the school yard. She looked around at the pictures on the wall. They seemed very high and far away.

In a few minutes she got down off the bench. She tiptoed to an open door and looked into a big room. There was no one inside the room. Star walked in and looked around. The room had great big windows. It had a long low table and some little tables just the same height. There were a lot of little chairs, just the right size for Star. She walked around the room. In one corner there were some large wooden toys. There were three wagons, a truck, and two doll coaches. Sitting on chairs against the wall were some dolls. Star was sure that this lovely room was the kindergarten.

She moved to the far side of the room and there she found a wooden house. The house had three windows. Two were upstairs and one was downstairs. It had a little green door and green shutters.

Star looked at the side of the house and there were four more windows. Two were upstairs and two were downstairs. Then she looked at the other side. There was another green door.

Star peeked around the corner of the house to see what was in the back. She was surprised to find that the house had no back. She slid between the side walls of the house and the blackboard and crawled into the house. Star thought this was the nicest playhouse she had ever seen. She looked out of the windows. She opened the front door and stuck her hand out. She closed the front door and opened the side door. When she closed it, she settled herself on the floor of the house. She didn't quite fill the house, but almost.

Just then Star heard a loud bell ringing and a great many feet running. She stayed very still and looked out of the second-story window. She thought it was great fun to sit on the first floor and look out of the second-story window. It made her feel like a giant.

In a few moments she saw Miss Morse come into the room. She was leading the line of kindergarten children. There was Rosemary at the head of the line. Farther along she could see Rickie and then Lillybell, and at the very end there was Polly.

"Sit down, boys and girls," said Miss Morse. "Don't shove, Toni. The chairs are all alike. Here, Lillybell, bring yours over beside me."

Star watched the children putting their chairs in a circle.

"Now," said Miss Morse, "we are going to learn a little song."

Meanwhile, Star's mother and Miss Preston walked out of the office. They were still talking about the parents' meeting. They walked through the hall and stopped just inside of the front door.

"Good-bye, Miss Preston," said Mother. "I'll see you at the meeting."

"Good-bye," said Miss Preston. "Thank you for coming." Then she added, "You have the papers I gave you, haven't you?"

"Yes, indeed," said Mother, looking under her arm. "I have everything. I haven't forgotten anything."

Star's mother ran down the steps and got into the car. She was busy thinking about the marketing that she must do. When she reached

the market, she parked the car in a big park-ing lot and went into the store.

Back in the kindergarten Miss Morse was playing the piano and the children were sing-ing. They all knew the song now. Even Star knew it, but she was singing it in a very soft voice inside the snug little house.

Miss Morse rose from the piano bench and said, "That was very good, boys and girls. You learned that song quickly. Now every-one may have a piece of paper and some crayons and we'll make pictures."

The children jumped up. They crowded around Miss Morse while she handed out pieces of paper and the crayons.

Star watched through the window of the

house. She wished she could have a piece of paper and some crayons. But it was fun to hide, she thought. She could see everybody and nobody could see her.

When Star's mother finished her marketing, she put the big bag of groceries in the car and drove home. Just as she opened the front door, she remembered Star. "Goodness gracious!" she said aloud. "Where is Star?"

Then she thought, "Why, I left her on the bench in the hall at school. But she wasn't there when I came out. I wonder where she can be."

Mother put the big bag of groceries on the kitchen table and ran back to the car. She jumped in quickly and drove to school. When she reached the school, she went into the principal's office.

"Miss Preston," she said, "have you seen Star? I drove off without her. I forgot that she came with me."

"Well, she must be around here somewhere," said Miss Preston. "I haven't seen her, but let's look for her."

"I left her sitting on the bench," said Star's mother. "Where do you suppose she went?"

Miss Preston walked up the hall and around the corner. The halls were empty. "Perhaps she's in the school yard," she said.

They went out and looked in the school yard but there was no one in sight.

"Where is the kindergarten?" said Star's mother.

"Right over here," replied Miss Preston, leading the way to the door of the kindergarten room. She opened the door and they walked into the room.

"Miss Morse," said Miss Preston, "have you seen anything of Betsy's little sister, Star?"

"Why, no!" said Miss Morse. "I haven't seen her."

Then she said to the children, "Have any of you boys and girls seen little Star?"

"You mean Twinkle," said Rickie.

"I saw her yesterday," said Lillybell.

"Yes, I know. We all saw her yesterday," said Miss Morse.

Star sat very still inside the house. Looking out through the little windows she could see her mother. She didn't know whether to come out of the house or stay inside. She guessed she would stay inside. It was fun to hide. It was fun to be in kindergarten and not have anyone know. She heard her mother say, "Well, it's very strange. Where ever could she have gone?"

"Perhaps she's upstairs with Betsy," said

Miss Preston. "You wait here and I'll go up and see."

Star saw Miss Preston go out of the room. She watched her mother talking to Miss Morse.

"Maybe Star's lost again," said Lillybell. "She was lost yesterday."

"Maybe the milkman will bring her," said Polly.

Just then Miss Preston returned. "She isn't up there," she said. "Betsy says she hasn't seen her."

"Well, thank you, Miss Preston," Star heard her mother say. "I'll have to look for her."

Star watched her mother walk toward the door. She watched her as she went out. Suddenly Star felt all shut in. Mother was leaving her! She was leaving her inside a big box.

The children had turned back to their papers and crayons. Suddenly from out of the little house there was a scream. "Mother! Mother! Wait for me, Mother!"

Miss Morse rushed across the room to the little house. All the children jumped up. Miss Morse pulled the house away from the blackboard and looked inside. There was Star, on her hands and knees. She was crying, "Mother! Wait for me!"

"Why, Star!" cried Miss Morse. "How did you get in there?"

But Star didn't answer. She scrambled to her feet and ran after her mother.

Mother had heard her. She came hurrying back up the steps of the school. At the front door Star ran into her mother's arms.

"Star! Star! Where have you been?" she said.

"I've been in the little house," said Star.

Star took hold of her mother's hand and they walked down the steps and across the street to the car. When they were settled in the front seat, Mother said, "It was very naughty of you to hide from Mother."

"I wasn't hiding from you, Mother. I was just hiding from the kindergarten."

"Oh!" said Mother. "What were you doing in the little house?"

"I was singing," said Star.

That evening when Father came home Star said, "Father, do you want to hear me sing a new song?"

"Yes, indeed!" said Father. "I'd love to hear you sing a new song.

This is the song she sang:

> *"I pulled the curtain back tonight,*
> *And there, so high and far,*
> *I saw the jolly, twinkly face*
> *Of my own special star.*
> *It always seems to tell me,*
> *That special star of mine,*
> *'We two know a big secret,*
> *That stars are meant to shine!'"*

"Where did you learn that song, Star?" Father asked.

"In kindergarten," said Star.

"In kindergarten!" exclaimed Father. "I didn't know you went to kindergarten."

"Well, I don't, 'zactly," said Star.

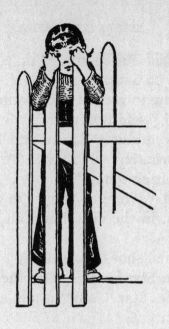

CHAPTER III

Star's Red Shoes

One morning Star was swinging on the front gate when Rosemary went by on her way to school.

"Are you coming to kindergarten again today, Star?" she asked.

"Not today," said Star. "I'm going to the city with my mother. I'm going to get new shoes."

"Oh," said Rosemary, "I'm going to get new shoes on Saturday."

"I'm going to get red ones," said Star.

"So am I," said Rosemary.

In a few minutes Rickie and Polly came by. "Hi, Twinkle!" said Rickie. "Are you going to kindergarten today?"

"Not today," replied Star. "I'm going to get new shoes. In the city. I'm going to get red shoes."

"I have red shoes," said Polly.

Just then Star heard her mother calling to her. "Come, Star. Come in and get ready to go to the city."

Star ran into the house and up the stairs.

"Can I come home from the city in my new red shoes, Mother?" Star asked.

"I suppose so," said Mother. "Wear your black patent leather Mary Janes."

"What dress am I going to wear?" Star asked, as she took off the sunsuit she had been wearing.

"The red-and-white-striped one," said Mother.

Star opened her closet and looked at the row of dresses that hung on a rod. They were just low enough for her to reach. She took the red-and-white-striped one off the rod.

Mother handed her a clean white slip, and in a few minutes Star was buttoning the last button on her red-and-white-striped dress.

"I like this dress," said Star.

"So do I," said Mother. "You look like a peppermint stick."

"My new red shoes will be pretty with this dress," said Star.

"They certainly will," replied Mother.

Star followed her mother to the garage. "Are we going to drive in to the city or are we going on the train?" asked Star.

"We're going to leave the car at the station and go in on the train," said Mother.

"I'm glad," said Star. "I love to ride on the train."

When they reached the station, Mother parked the car. Then she took hold of Star's hand and they crossed the parking lot to the station platform. They sat down on a bench and waited for the train.

When the train came, the conductor lifted Star up the steps. Mother followed her into the car. They found an empty seat and Star sat by the window. She looked out of the window all the way to the city.

When they got off the train, Star skipped along beside her mother. Finally they turned into a very big store. They stepped into an elevator. When it stopped at the fourth floor, Mother said, "Step out, Star."

Star stepped out and Mother followed. They walked past some long benches. The benches were filled with ladies. They were all trying on shoes. When Star and her mother reached the far corner, they sat down. This was the children's shoe department.

"Sit right here, beside me," said Mother.

Star sat down. She squirmed herself back until her back rested against the bench. Her legs stuck out straight before her.

In a few minutes a man came over to where Star and her mother were sitting. He sat down on a little stool in front of them and said, "What can I do for you?"

Mother said, "I would like to have a pair of red shoes for my little girl."

The man took Star's shoes off. Then he picked up a piece of wood and put it under Star's foot. "This is to see what size you take," he said.

The man walked away. Star saw him disappear behind a high wall made of lots and lots of shoe boxes.

In a few minutes he returned. "I'm sorry," he said, "but we have no red shoes for the little lady. We're sold out. I can give you brown only."

"No, thank you," said Mother. "We want red ones, don't we, Star?"

"Yes," said Star. "We want red ones."

Star and her mother went to another store. They went to many other stores, but none of them had red shoes to fit Star.

Finally Mother said, "Well, darling, I guess we shall have to buy you a pair of brown shoes."

Star's eyes filled with tears. "But I wanted red ones," she said.

"I know you did," said Mother, "but we can't get them.

"We'll have them in later," said the salesman.

"But she needs shoes now," said Mother. "Try the brown ones on."

Star blinked hard to keep back the tears as she tried on the brown shoes.

"Don't be a baby, Star," said her mother. "You can have red shoes the next time."

"But I wanted them this time."

"Well, we can't always have everything we want, dear," said Mother.

Star looked at the brown shoes on her feet. She didn't care now whether she had new shoes or not. She walked up and down in the brown shoes. When Mother asked her if they were comfortable, she said, "I guess so."

"Do you want to wear them home, dear?" Mother asked.

Star shook her head. "I don't think so," she replied.

"You had better send them," she heard her mother say to the salesman.

As they waited for the elevator, Mother said to Star, "Now, darling, I have a lot of shopping to do. There is a playroom on the top floor. Let's go up and see if you would like to stay there while I finish the rest of the shopping."

The elevator shot up to the top floor. When they stepped out, they walked across the floor to a doorway that had a low gate. Star looked over the gate and saw some boys and girls, just about her own age. Two were playing in a big sandbox. One was riding on a rocking horse, and three were sitting at a long table making pictures with crayons.

"Why, it's a kindergarten!" exclaimed Star.

"Yes, it is, dear," said Mother. "Would you like to stay here until Mother is through?"

"Oh, yes!" said Star.

A lady came over to the gate and said, "Would your little girl like to come in and stay with us?"

"Yes, I believe she would," said Mother. "My little girl's name is Star."

"But they call me Twinkle in kindergarten," said Star.

"Well, Twinkle, we'll be happy to have you. My name is Miss Green."

Miss Green opened the gate and Star walked into the room.

"I'll be back for you," said Mother, turning away. "I promise I won't forget you today."

The boy in the sandbox looked at Star. "What's her name?" he called out.

"Twinkle," said Miss Green. And then she said to Star, "His name is Sammy, and the little girl in the sandbox is Ruthie. Jack is riding on the rocking horse, and I'm sure he'll let you ride too."

"Not until I come back from Florida," said Jack. "I'm riding this horse to Florida."

Miss Green led Star to the table. "And here are David and Lynn and Susan. Would you like to draw with crayons, Star?"

"I would like to play in the sandbox," said Star.

"Very well," said Miss Green. "You can play in the sandbox."

Star got in the sandbox with Sammy and Ruthie. "We're making a superhighway," said Sammy.

"For these automobiles," said Ruthie, holding up a toy automobile.

"You can help if you want to," said Sammy.

Star set to work on the superhighway.

"You're not making it smooth enough," said Sammy. "The cars will bounce if it isn't smooth."

"I guess I'll make some sand pies," said Star, picking up a mold shaped like a fish.

"I thought you were going to help with the superhighway," said Sammy.

"I don't like to make superhighways," said Star. "I like to make sand pies."

After a while Star climbed out of the sandbox and went over to the table where the other children were working. She was just about to make a picture with crayons when Miss Green put some empty glass jars on the table.

"If anyone would like to make a flower vase," she said, "here are some glass jars and here are some cans of paint."

The children stopped drawing with crayons. Sammy and Ruthie came out of the sandbox. Jack came back from Florida like a rocket. He climbed off the rocking horse. They all wanted to paint flower vases.

Miss Green brought the cans of paint from the closet. "Now, this is sticky paint," she said. "And it dries very quickly. Be careful not to spill it."

While Miss Green was spreading newspapers on the long table, she said, "There are some painting aprons hanging on a hook in the closet. Everyone must put on a painting apron."

The children went to the closet and each one put on a painting apron.

"I want to make a red one," said Star.

"I do too," said David.

"Well, then, you'll have to share the can of red paint," said Miss Green, as she spread some newspapers on the floor.

"Now stand on the newspapers," she said.

The children stood on the newspapers. Soon they were all at work. Each one had an empty glass jar and a paintbrush. The paint flowed on smoothly. They were turning the glass jars into bright-colored flower vases.

Star was about half finished when suddenly David knocked the can of red paint right off the table. Star quickly bent forward to keep the paint from going down the front of her apron. The can of paint landed right at her feet. The red paint splashed all over her shoes.

As soon as Miss Green saw what had happened, she came running with a big cloth. "Oh, my goodness!" she cried. "Twinkle, look at your shoes. Here, let me wipe the paint off them. We must do it quickly before it dries."

Star stood staring down at her feet. She was standing in a puddle of bright red paint, and her shoes were the color of a fire engine. The red paint had splashed all over them.

Miss Green stooped down. "No, no!" cried Star. "Don't wipe it off. Please don't wipe it off. I like them that way." Star began jumping up and down.

"Oh, be still!" said Miss Green. "You'll get paint all over the floor."

"Well, don't wipe it off. Please don't wipe it off," said Star.

"But your mother will be very angry," said Miss Green.

"No, she won't," said Star. "She wants me to have red shoes."

The paint on Star's shoes dried very quickly and nothing could be done about them. Miss Green gathered up the newspapers from the floor. There was just enough paint left in the can to finish painting the two vases.

When Star's mother returned, the only sign of the mess that David had made with the red paint was Star's shoes.

Star ran to meet her mother. "Look, Mother!" she cried. "I have red shoes." Then as she looked at the backs of her shoes and the heels, which were still black, she added, "Almost."

"We had an accident," said Miss Green, "but Star wouldn't let me wipe the paint off her shoes. I am very sorry."

"Well, it certainly is a good thing you didn't have the new shoes on, Star," said her mother. "Those shoes look dreadful."

"Oh, no, Mother!" cried Star. "They're beautiful."

Star trotted off in her funny shoes, red in the front and black in the back. But when she looked down at her feet she only saw the fronts, and she thought they looked pretty.

When Rosemary came to play with her just before dinner, Star said, "See my red shoes, Rosemary."

Rosemary looked at Star's shoes and said,

"They're the funniest red shoes I ever saw."

"But they're red shoes," said Star.

"Well," said Rosemary, "they're not the kind of red shoes I want."

CHAPTER IV

Billy's Halloween Party

It was Halloween and Betsy was dressing for a party. Billy Porter, who was in Betsy's class in school, was giving the party.

On Betsy's bed sat a little dwarf with a long gray beard. He was wearing dark green breeches and a little brown velvet jacket. On his head was a pointed hat, and his brown shoes had long pointed toes that turned up at the ends. The little dwarf's face was very sad. Every few minutes he would sob and then he

43

would sniffle. "Sob-sniffle! Sob-sniffle!" went the little dwarf.

Finally Betsy said, "Oh, Twinkle, don't cry. You'll go to a party when you're a bigger girl."

"I want to go to a party now," said Star, who was the little dwarf sitting on Betsy's bed. "I'm all dressed up for Halloween and I can't go to a party."

"But there are plenty of boys and girls who aren't going to the party," said Betsy. "Even Eddie Wilson isn't going to the party, and he's much bigger than you are."

Betsy was putting on her costume. She put on a long black skirt and a black cape. Then she put a tall, pointed black hat on her head. When she put on her false face she looked horrible, for now she was an old witch with a hooked nose and a grinning mouth with only one tooth. When Betsy turned and faced Star, the little dwarf leapt from the bed and ran out of the room screaming loud screams.

"What's the matter?" said Mother, as Star ran into her in the hall.

"It's Betsy!" cried Star. "She's an old witch!"

Betsy laughed behind her false face. "Don't I look wonderful, Mother?" she said.

"You certainly look horrible," said Mother.

Now that Star had hold of her mother's hand she wasn't afraid. "You're going to scare everybody at the party, Betsy," she said. She began to wish once more that she could go to the party. "I wish I could go to the party," she said.

"Father is going to take you over to Lillybell's house," said Mother, "and you can both go in to see Mrs. Jackson. I think she'll have some cookies for you."

Just then Mr. Wilson drove up in his car. In the back of his car he had a clown and a cowboy, an Indian and a fairy. They were some of the boys and girls who were going to Billy's party. The clown and the cowboy were the Wilson twins, Joe and Frank.

When Betsy came out of the house, Joe cried, "Oh! Look at the old witch!"

Betsy climbed into the front seat with Mr. Wilson.

"Oh, Betsy," cried Frank, "Eddie's mad because he wasn't invited to the party! He locked himself in the cellar."

"Why did he do that?" Betsy asked.

"Oh, Eddie's always doing something in the cellar," said Joe. "He has a lot of junk down there."

"Isn't he going to get dressed up?" Betsy asked.

"He wouldn't tell," said Joe. "He just kept saying he'd show everybody, he'd scare everybody stiff."

All the children shouted with glee. "I'd like to see him scare me," said the Indian.

"Me too," said Joe and Frank in a chorus.

In the meantime Father drove Star around to Lillybell's house. Lillybell was dressed like a bride. She was wearing a long white dress and her mother had fastened a piece of an old lace curtain on her head. She had on white gloves and carried a bunch of white paper flowers. Her false face had long curly eyelashes, which Lillybell thought were very beautiful.

"Now, don't you come with us, Father," said Star. "'Cause if you do, Mrs. Jackson will know who we are."

"Very well!" replied Father. "I'll wait right here in the car for you."

The little dwarf with the long gray beard and the bride with the curly eyelashes walked up the steps to Mrs. Jackson's porch. They walked to the front door. The doorbell was

too high for them to reach, so they knocked on the door with their fists.

No one came to the door.

They both leaned against the door and pounded again. Suddenly the door was pulled open and the bride and the little dwarf fell in. The bride got all tangled up in her lace veil and the dwarf's beard came loose.

"My goodness!" cried Mr. Jackson, who had pulled open the door. "What have we here?"

Mrs. Jackson came running. "What's the matter?" she cried, looking down at the wriggling dwarf and bride.

"Looks like a bride and groom here," said Mr. Jackson.

"No, no!" cried the dwarf, getting up. "I'm not a groom. I'm a dwarf."

"Of course!" said Mr. Jackson. "Of course you're a dwarf. I can tell by your beard, which, by the way, is lying on the floor."

Mr. Jackson picked up the beard. "Come here," he said. "Let me see if I can fasten it on for you."

"You don't know who I am, do you?" said Star.

"Now, let me see," said Mr. Jackson. "Are you Lillybell?"

"No!" Star laughed and pointed to the bride, who was being helped up by Mrs. Jackson. "She's Lillybell!"

"So that's Lillybell!" said Mr. Jackson, tying on the dwarf's beard.

"Oh, you shouldn't have told him," said Lillybell.

"They don't know who I am," said Star.

"You wouldn't be the little girl who lives on the other side of our garden wall, would you?" said Mr. Jackson.

"Is her name Twinkle?" asked the little dwarf.

"No, I don't believe that's her name," said Mr. Jackson.

"Is it Star?" said the dwarf.

"Doesn't sound like that," said Mr. Jackson.

"Yes, it is!" cried Star. "I'm Star and I'm Twinkle too."

"Well, what do you know about that?" said Mr. Jackson. "I never would have guessed it."

Mrs. Jackson was passing a plate of ginger cookies. Star and Lillybell had to take off their false faces in order to eat the cookies.

After they had finished their cookies, they said good-bye to Mr. and Mrs. Jackson and went back to the car.

"Now how would you like to call on Mrs. Wilson?" Father asked.

"All right," said Star.

Again Father stayed in the car while the children knocked on the front door. They waited and knocked again.

At last they heard footsteps. The door was opened with a swish by what looked to Star and Lillybell like a flock of ghosts, led by a horrible white skeleton.

"Oh! Oh! Oh!" they shrieked. Star raced back to the car, followed by Lillybell, tripping all the way over her long white dress.

"Hey!" shouted the voice of little Eddie Wilson. "Hey! Wait!"

Star was kneeling on the seat of the car with her face hidden against her father's shoulder. Lillybell was hiding her face against Star's back.

"Hey!" cried Eddie, as he reached the car. "They're just balloons. Come on in. I need you."

Star heard her father laugh, so she turned and peeked out between her fingers at Eddie.

Eddie was standing by the car, holding three balloons. Two were white with eyes and nose and mouth painted on them with black paint.

Each balloon was draped in a white cheese-cloth duster. With the moonlight shining on them and the wind blowing the white dusters, they looked like very scary ghosts. The other balloon was black. It had a white paper skeleton head pasted on it.

"I'm going over to the party at Billy Porter's," said Eddie, "and I'm going to scare the crowd out of their wits. Only, I have to have somebody to help me."

"I'll help you," said Lillybell. But she said it in a very small voice, because she was still a little bit scared.

"I'll help you too," said Star.

"Well," said Eddie, "I guess there isn't anybody else. My big brother Rudy went over to his scout meeting. Papa's gone to see a friend of his and Mama's talking on the telephone."

Then Eddie looked up at Star's father and said, "Please, will you take me over to Billy Porter's house? I'd 'preciate it a lot."

"Well," said Star's father, "I guess if you can't play pranks on Halloween, it isn't Halloween. Come along."

Eddie climbed into the back of the car with his balloons. Star and Lillybell sat on the front seat.

On the way to Billy's house Eddie told them his plan. "The party is going to be in the Porters' living room," said Eddie. "The living room has three windows and I'm going to scare them at all three windows. But I can't do it all by myself." Then Eddie told Star and Lillybell what they were to do. When he finished he said, "Now, do you understand?"

"Oh, yes!" said the bride and the dwarf together.

When they reached Billy Porter's house, they got out of the car. Eddie handed Star and Lillybell each a ghost balloon.

Star's father tied each little girl's balloon to her wrist. "Now take hold of the string, right close to the balloon," he said. "And remember, when you get under the window, let go of the string. Then the balloon will float up outside the window. It won't get away from you, because the end of the string is tied to your wrist."

"I know how to do it," said Star, as she tiptoed toward the house.

"Sh!" said Eddie. "Don't let them go until you hear me tap on the window."

"Okay!" said Lillybell.

The children were very close to the house now. They could hear the boys and girls inside shouting and laughing. They sounded as though they were playing games. Suddenly all the lights went out. The children in the house shrieked. Someone inside the house was trying to scare them too. It was a perfect time for Eddie's trick.

At this moment Star and Lillybell and Eddie were each crouching below one of the living-room windows. Star's father was beside her.

Eddie reached up and tapped on the window. Immediately the three balloons bobbed up. The wind whipped the cheesecloth dusters around and Eddie pulled his skeleton up and down.

"Look! Look!" someone cried out.

"Oh!" "Eeek!" "Oh-h-h!" Wild shrieks came from inside the house.

Eddie and Star and Lillybell laughed and laughed and so did Star's father.

"That scared 'em," said Eddie.

In a few minutes the front door was opened and Mr. Porter looked out. When he saw who was outside he called, "Come in, ghosties. You've just about scared this crowd silly."

"I told you I would," said Eddie as he walked into the house.

When Betsy saw Star and Lillybell, she said, "How did you babies get into this?"

"We came to help Eddie scare you," said Lillybell.

And just then Mrs. Porter began serving ice cream.

Star fell sound asleep on her father's lap before she had finished hers. Mr. Porter had to carry Lillybell out to the car. She, too, was sound asleep. The ghost balloons were still tied to the wrists of the little dwarf with the long gray beard and the bride with the curly eyelashes.

CHAPTER V

How Koala Bear Went to Kindergarten

Koala Bear lay under a pile of brown leaves. Koala was lying under the leaves because that is where Star had left him. She had been playing in the pile of leaves that Father had made when he raked the front lawn. She had made believe that she was a mama bear and that Koala was a baby bear and that they were going to spend the winter buried under the leaves. She was cozily settled, with only her tiny button of a nose sticking out, when she heard a car stop in front of the house.

She lifted her head and saw that it was Father. She watched him as he got out of the car and walked to the back of it. There he unlocked the trunk compartment and lifted the door. She wondered what Father had inside. Her eyes grew larger and larger as she saw him lift out a brand-new tricycle.

Star jumped out of her bed of leaves and dashed toward the car. "Oh, Father!" she cried. "Is that for me?"

"You little snooper," said Father. "Where were you hiding? This was supposed to be a surprise."

"Oh, it is!" cried Star. "I'm awfully surprised. May I ride it right away?"

"You can't ride it until I unwrap the wheels and the handlebars," said Father, tearing the brown paper away.

Star was jumping up and down, she was so excited.

In a few minutes the paper was off and the shiny red tricycle was standing in front of

Star. Star was on the seat in a flash. Off she went, pedaling faster and faster. At the corner she turned around and rode back to Father. Her face was shining like a sunbeam.

"Well!" said Father. "I guess you like it."

"I love it!" shouted Star as she dashed past Father.

Father went into the house. Star rode up and down and around the block until Mother called her to come in to dinner.

Star wheeled the tricycle up the drive and around to the back door. "I have to bring my tricycle in the house," she said. "It's too nice to leave in the garage."

Betsy held the door open while Star and her mother lifted the tricycle up the two steps.

"Isn't it pretty, Mother?" asked Star.

"It certainly is," replied Mother.

"It's just as pretty as my two-wheeler," said Betsy.

After supper Star rode the tricycle around the kitchen until Mother chased her off to bed. While she undressed, she talked to Betsy about the tricycle until Betsy said, "Star, how can I do my lessons with you talking about the tricycle? Do be quiet."

Finally Mother came and tucked her into bed. She said her prayers in a very sleepy voice, and in a still sleepier voice she said, "The bell on my tricycle is nice and loud."

In a moment she was asleep. It was the first night since she had had him that Star had gone to bed without Koala Bear. He lay outside in the pile of leaves. He lay there all night.

In the morning an Airedale, out for an early-morning walk, came in through the open gate. He smelled around the bushes. He smelled around the faded flower beds. He poked his nose into the pile of leaves and uncovered Koala Bear. He sniffed Koala all over. Then he poked him with his nose.

The next moment he had Koala between his jaws and was trotting down the street. He carried Koala very gently. Down the street he went and around the corner. He crossed the street, went up the street, around the corner, across another street, and kept on until finally he turned into the path leading up to his own front door.

But he didn't stop at the front door. Instead, he walked over to a flower bed beside the door. It was filled with the withered stalks

of what had been the summer plants. There
he dug a hole in the soft earth. He dropped
Koala into the hole. When he finished he
walked over to the front door, scratched it,
and said, "Arf!"

In a moment the door was opened by a
little girl. Her name was Cathy Collins. When
she saw the dog she called out, "Oh, Mummy!

Brownie's been digging again. His nose is all covered with dirt."

"Oh, dear," said her mother. "I do wish that dog would stop burying things. He buries everything, even his dog biscuits."

Two days later, a gardener came to Cathy's house to fix the flower beds for the winter. With a rake he raked all the leaves out of the flower beds. When he reached the flower bed beside the front door, he cut the dried stalks off the plants. Then he raked out the leaves. He was almost finished when the rake caught on Koala Bear's ear and rolled him over. The gardener stooped down and picked him up.

"Well, well!" said the gardener, brushing the dirt off Koala. "Such a place to leave a toy! It's no wonder they get lost." He sat Koala on the step by the front door and went on with his work.

There Koala sat until Cathy's father came home from work. When he saw the little bear sitting by the front door, he picked him up and carried him inside. "Such a place to leave a toy!" he muttered. "No wonder they get lost. Just dropped all over the place."

Mr. Collins carried Koala Bear upstairs to Cathy's bedroom. He sat him down on the windowsill in the midst of Cathy's dolls.

That night when Cathy was getting ready for bed, she walked to the windowsill to look over her family. The first thing that her eye fell upon was Koala Bear. She was much surprised to see him sitting on the lap of Ollie, her best doll.

Cathy picked him up and looked at him carefully. Then she called to her mother, "Mummy! There's a bear in my room."

"Don't be silly, Cathy," her mother called back. "Just get into bed."

"But there is," cried Cathy, carrying Koala to the head of the stairs. "He only has one ear."

"Now, Cathy," her mother called up, "I want this nonsense to stop. It's time for you to be in bed. You won't be able to get up in the morning to go to kindergarten."

"But, Mummy," said Cathy, "there *is* a bear here. Mayn't I bring him down to show you?"

"You may not come downstairs, Cathy," said her mother. "You are to get into bed and stop being silly. There is no bear up there."

Mr. Collins was sitting by the fire reading

the evening paper. Suddenly he became aware of what Cathy's mother had said. He lowered the paper with a rustle and said, "Oh, but there is a bear up there!"

Mrs. Collins' mouth opened in surprise. She looked at Cathy's father and said, "Now, are you going to be silly too?"

"I'm not being silly," he replied. "I found a toy bear sitting outside the front door. I carried it upstairs and put it on Cathy's windowsill. Isn't it hers?"

"Oh!" said Mrs. Collins, and mounted the stairs.

She found Cathy sitting on her bed, looking at Koala Bear.

"See, Mummy!" said Cathy. "You didn't believe me."

"I'm sorry, Cathy," said her mother. "I didn't understand."

Cathy handed the bear to her mother, and Mrs. Collins said, "Where do you suppose it came from? Daddy says he found it sitting on our front steps."

"I don't know," said Cathy. "He's a nice little bear, even though he only has one ear."

"You'd better take him to kindergarten to-

morrow," said her mother. "Perhaps he belongs to one of the children who goes to
kindergarten."

"But why can't he belong to me?" Cathy
asked. "I like him very much."

"But he isn't your bear," said her mother,
"and I'm sure the boy or girl to whom he
belongs would like to have him back."

"Well, that boy or girl ought to take better
care of their bear," said Cathy, "and not leave
him sitting on people's steps."

"Never mind," said her mother. "Let me
tuck you into bed. You can take the little
bear to kindergarten in the morning."

Cathy rolled over on the bed with Koala in
her arms. Mother heard her prayers and tucked
the covers around her. That night Koala slept
in a strange bed.

The next morning Cathy carried Koala to
kindergarten. She showed him to Miss Morse
and all the children. When Lillybell saw him
she cried out, "Why, that's Koala Bear! He
belongs to Star."

"Are you sure?" Miss Morse asked.

"Yes, Miss Morse," said Lillybell. "That
sure is Koala Bear."

"Well, we'll put him over here with the

other toys for today," said Miss Morse. "When you see Star, Lillybell, you can ask her if she lost her toy bear."

At noontime when Lillybell was walking home from kindergarten, she saw Star riding her tricycle in front of her house.

"Star!" Lillybell sang out. "Koala Bear is in kindergarten."

Star stopped riding and looked at Lillybell. She didn't say a word. She was thinking of Koala Bear for the first time since Father had brought the tricycle home.

She climbed off the tricycle and ran to the pile of leaves. She got down on her hands and knees and crawled all through the leaves, but she couldn't find Koala Bear.

Then she got up and ran into the house. "Mother!" she cried. "Koala Bear is in kindergarten! Mother! Koala Bear is in kindergarten! I have to go to kindergarten and get Koala Bear."

"However did Koala Bear get to kindergarten?" said Mother.

"I don't know," said Star. "I left him buried in the leaves, but Lillybell says Koala Bear is in kindergarten."

"Well, we'll drive over and get Betsy this afternoon when school is over," said Mother. "Then you can see if Koala Bear is in kindergarten."

Star could hardly wait for three o'clock to come, she was so anxious to go to kindergarten to get Koala Bear. Lillybell was riding the tricycle, but Star didn't mind. She just kept running to her mother, asking her if it wasn't almost time to go.

At last the time arrived to get the car out of the garage. Star hopped in beside her mother, and off they went to the school.

When they arrived, Star ran up the steps of the school ahead of her mother. The door was too heavy for Star, so she had to wait for Mother to pull it open. She ran on her tiptoes to the kindergarten room. She took hold of the doorknob and pulled. The door was locked.

Star's heart was beating fast and tears rose in her eyes. She turned an anxious face up to her mother. "It's locked," she said.

Mother looked through the glass in the door. It was too high for Star.

"Do you see him, Mother?" asked Star. "Do you see Koala Bear?"

"No, I don't see him," said her mother, "but we'll go and ask Miss Preston about it."

Star trotted off beside her mother. When they entered the principal's office, Mother said, "Miss Preston, we have heard that Star's Koala Bear is in the kindergarten. We don't know how he got there, but Lillybell says she saw him there."

"Well," said Miss Preston, "I'll unlock the door and we'll see."

Miss Preston took a key from a hook, and Star followed her mother and Miss Preston down the hall to the door of the kindergarten.

Miss Preston turned the key in the lock and

pulled the door open. Star walked into the quiet room. The little chairs stood in tidy rows and the tables were bare. She looked all around the room, and there, sitting on a doll's chair, she saw Koala Bear.

Star rushed to him and picked him up. "Oh, Koala," she said. "Koala Bear! How did you get here?"

But Koala didn't say anything, because he was just a little toy bear and couldn't talk.

When Star was seated in the car between her mother and Betsy, she held Koala on her lap. "Just think," she said. "Koala Bear was in kindergarten all morning. But he didn't know he was in kindergarten, did he, Mother?"

"I'm afraid he didn't," replied Mother.

Star let out a deep sigh. "I wish I could go to kindergarten," she said, " 'cause I'd know I was there."

CHAPTER VI

Star Finds a New Friend

One morning Star was looking at Koala Bear, who was sitting on the breakfast table staring into Star's dish of cereal.

"Mother," said Star, "how do you suppose Koala Bear got to kindergarten?"

"Well, Star, if you left Koala buried in the leaves, I think some dog must have carried him off. But how Koala reached kindergarten I don't know," her mother replied.

Star's face was very serious and her eyes

grew big. She nodded her head. "I'll bet that was just what happened. Some dog carried Koala away."

Star sat thinking of this for a few minutes and then she said, "And I'll bet I know what dog it was. I'll bet it was that Scottie dog. Have you seen that Scottie dog, Mother?"

"I don't believe I have," said Mother. "To whom does the Scottie dog belong?"

"I don't know," said Star, "but he's a very nasty dog. The first time I saw him was yesterday. He's a nasty dog. He bites."

"How do you know he bites?" Mother asked. "Did you ever see him bite anyone?"

"No," said Star. "But he would bite if he had anybody to bite."

"Oh, I don't think so," said Mother. "He's probably a very nice little dog."

"He barks at Thumpy terrible," said Star.

"Well, Thumpy probably barks at him," said Mother. "Thumpy can certainly do his share of barking."

"But the Scottie starts it," said Star.

She had no sooner said this than a great commotion broke out in front of the house. Thumpy seemed to be barking his head off.

Star got up from the breakfast table and

ran to the front door. She opened it. There was Thumpy rushing back and forth along the white picket fence, barking as loud as ever he could bark.

On the other side of the fence there was a Scottie dog running back and forth and barking just as loud as Thumpy.

"Thumpy!" cried Star. "Thumpy! Come away from that nasty dog!"

Thumpy paid no attention to Star. He kept right on rushing from one end of the fence to the other and he kept right on barking.

Star shouted, "Go away, you nasty Scottie. Go away."

The barking continued.

Star leaned down and picked up a sharp stone. She threw it with all her might at the Scottie, but instead of hitting the Scottie it hit Thumpy. With a yelp of pain Thumpy ran away from the fence. He ran to the back of the house and got under a big bush. There he lay whimpering and whining.

Star ran after him, crying, "Oh, Thumpy, Thumpy!"

When she found him under the bush, she got down on her hands and knees and crawled under to him. Then she saw that the stone had hit Thumpy on his left eye. His eye was closed. "Oh, Thumpy!" she moaned.

Star pulled him out from under the bush. By this time she was sobbing over Thumpy. She tried to pick him up, but he lay like a stone at her feet. "I didn't mean to, Thumpy," she sobbed. "I didn't mean to do it."

Thumpy rolled his one good eye up and whimpered.

Star tried again to lift him. Finally she had him in her arms. He was very heavy, but she managed to carry him to the back door. She kicked her foot against the door and cried out, "Mother! Mother! Open the door. Please open the door."

Mother opened the door and looked down at Star with Thumpy in her arms.

"Oh, Mother! Thumpy's hurt," cried Star. "His eye is hurt."

Mother took Thumpy from Star and carried him into the house. She sat down on a chair with Thumpy in her lap. She looked at his eye and said, "Why, how did that happen?"

The tears were rolling down Star's face. "It was that Scottie dog," she sobbed. "That Scottie dog made me hit Thumpy with a stone. He made me hit Thumpy in the eye. He's a

nasty Scottie dog. He stole Koala Bear and now look what he did to Thumpy!"

"Be quiet, Star," said Mother, as she put Thumpy down and left the room.

When Mother returned, she had a basin of cold water, and a cloth. "We'll just bathe Thumpy's eye with cold water," she said.

Mother and Star sat down on the floor beside Thumpy, and Mother bathed Thumpy's eye with the cold water. Thumpy rolled the other eye toward Mother and licked his nose.

"You see, Star," said Mother, "this is what happens when people throw stones. I have told you never to throw stones."

"It was that Scottie dog," said Star.

"No," replied Mother, "it was not the Scottie dog. It was you who threw the stone. You meant to hit the Scottie and that would have been just as bad as hitting Thumpy."

"But he's a nasty dog. He stole Koala Bear and he bites," said Star.

"You don't know whether the Scottie took Koala Bear," said her mother, "and you just think he bites. All you really know is that the Scottie barks. And all dogs bark. Thumpy barks."

"Do you think it hurts him very much?" Star asked.

"I hope not," said Mother.

"May I do it?" said Star.

Mother handed the rag to Star, and Star bathed Thumpy's eye. "It's a little bit open," she cried. "Is it getting better, Mother?"

"Yes, it's getting better," said Mother, "but I hope you will never throw another stone."

"I won't," said Star. "I didn't know stones hurt so much."

Star sat beside Thumpy almost all morning, bathing his eye. Thumpy was pleased. He had never had so much attention.

Once Star said, "Mother, who do you think owns that Scottie?"

"I don't know, dear," said Mother. "Perhaps he belongs to the people who have just moved near us."

By noontime Thumpy's eye was open again and he was as frisky as ever.

Star had scrambled eggs for her lunch and a dish of junket. Then she went out to ride her tricycle. Thumpy ran beside her as she rode down to the corner. Just as she reached the corner she met with a surprise. Another tricycle came around the corner and almost bumped into her. The tricycle was ridden by a little boy about her own age. He had red hair and big brown eyes. They both stopped and looked at each other. Thumpy began sniffing at the little boy's legs.

After a few minutes the boy said, "What's your name?"

"Twinkle," said Star.

"That's a funny name," said the little boy.

"I've got another one," said Star.

"What is it?" asked the boy.

"Star," said Star.

"Like up in the sky?" asked the boy.

"Yes," said Star. "What's your name?"

"Butch," said the boy. And like a flash he turned his tricycle and pedaled off.

Star turned and pedaled in the opposite direction. At the corner she went around the block. Thumpy ran beside her.

At the next corner she met Butch. Again they both stopped.

"What's her name?" said Butch, pointing to Thumpy.

"He isn't a her," said Star. "He's a him."

"Well, what's his name?" said Butch.

"Thumpy," said Star.

"I've got a dog," said Butch. "Her name is Joey."

"That's a boy's name," said Star.

"No it isn't," said Butch. "Her name is Josephine. We call her Joey."

"Oh," said Star. "Where do you live?"

"Right up there," said Butch, pointing to a house up the street. "We moved in there yesterday. Do you want to see Joey?"

"All right," said Star.

Star and Butch rode up the street side by side. Finally they reached a house where a lady was sweeping the front step. "Mother!" Butch called out. "This is Twinkle Star. She's my friend. She wants to see Joey."

Butch whistled, and out of the front door bounded the Scottie dog. She ran up to Butch and then she ran to Thumpy. They didn't bark at all. They just began to play together.

Star watched them in surprise. Then she looked at Butch and said, "Do you go to kindergarten?"

"No," said Butch.

"How old are you?" Star asked.

"I'm four," said Butch.

Without another word Star set off on the tricycle as fast as she could go, right back to her own house.

She left the tricycle by the front gate and ran into the house. "Mother! Mother!" she called. "I've got somebody to play with. His name is Butch. He's the Scottie dog's father."

"My, what a lot of news!" exclaimed Mother.

"Her name is Joey, Mother. Only, it's something else. I forget. But she's awful cute, Mother. She's a friend of Thumpy's.''

Star ran out of the house again and jumped on her tricycle. She was going back to Butch.

CHAPTER VII

The Mailman Who Had Two Pockets

Star always knew when the mailman was coming down the street. The brown cocker spaniel who lived in the house on the corner would begin to bark. Then the fox terrier next door would begin to bark. At the same time Thumpy would give a low growl. Then he would lift his head high and bark. He would rush to the front door and fling himself against it, leaping and barking furiously. When the letters and papers came through the slot in the front door, Thumpy would growl like a wild tiger in the zoo.

If Thumpy happened to be in the front yard when the mailman came around the corner, he would run up and down along the white picket fence, barking his head off. Star and her mother would have to come out and take Thumpy by the collar and pull him into the house. Meanwhile, the mailman would stand by the gate, clicking his tongue and saying, "Don't know why people want to keep such fierce dogs. Fierce dogs all over the neighborhood. Not safe to deliver anything."

"He won't bite," said Star one day, as she dragged Thumpy away from the front gate.

"Well, I'm not taking any chances," said the mailman. "Maybe he won't bite me, but it sure looks as though he would like to taste me. And I don't want to be tasted."

One morning Star saw letters lying on the floor by the front door. "Mother!" she called, as she picked them up. "Here are some letters."

"I'm surprised that he left them, with

Thumpy in the yard," said her mother.

Star opened the front door and called to Thumpy. He came in licking his chops.

"Oh, Mother!" cried Star. "Thumpy's licking his mouth. He's licking his mouth, Mother. Do you think he tasted the mailman?"

"I don't believe so," said Mother. "The mailman must have been feeling brave this morning."

Star ran to the gate and looked up the street, but the mailman was nowhere in sight.

The following morning Star and Butch were in the yard with Thumpy when the mailman came around the corner. He was whistling a tune.

"Woof!" said the brown cocker spaniel at the corner.

"Woof!" said the fox terrier next door.

"Woof!" said Thumpy, running to the fence.

But none of the dogs barked. Instead, they wagged their tails.

When the mailman reached the house next door, Star saw that he was not the mailman who had always brought the letters before. This was another man. He walked quickly and he had a merry twinkle in his eye. As he opened the next-door gate, he winked at Star and Butch. He stopped whistling and said, "Hello, there! How are you this morning?"

"Fine," said Butch.

"I'm fine too," said Star, as she watched the fox terrier run to the mailman, sniffing.

The mailman put out his hand and said, "Hi, there, feller!" Then he dropped the letters through the slot in the front door.

In a moment the mailman was at Star's front gate. Thumpy ran to meet him. "Hiya, pal!" said the mailman to Thumpy, holding out his hand.

Star saw that the mailman was giving Thumpy something to eat. "What did you give Thumpy?" she asked.

"Just a piece of candy," the mailman told her.

"A piece of candy!" cried Butch.

"Do you give all the dogs a piece of candy?" Star asked.

"Certainly do," said the mailman. "It saves a lot of trouble. Do you want a piece too?"

"Oh, yes, please," said Star.

Star and Butch watched the mailman put his hand in his left pocket. "I keep the candy for the children in this pocket," he said. "They're wrapped in paper. Other pocket has the dog's candy—no wrappers."

The mailman handed a piece of candy wrapped in wax paper to each one of the children.

"Thank you!" said Star.

"Thanks!" said Butch.

"Quite welcome," said the mailman as he slipped the letters through the slot in the door.

"Are you going to be our mailman all the time?" asked Star.

"Looks that way," said the mailman.

"Do you bring the letters to our house?" Butch asked.

"Where is your house?" said the mailman.

"It's on Oak Road," replied Butch.

"Yes, I serve Oak Road," said the mailman.

"I'm glad," said Butch. "I have a Scottie dog. Her name is Joey."

"Think I gave Joey a piece of candy about a half hour ago," said the mailman.

"What time do you get to our house?" Butch asked.

"About half past nine," said the mailman as he closed the gate.

Star ran into the house to find her mother. "Mother!" she cried. "We have a new mailman. He gives all the dogs candy and he gave Butch and me candy too."

"Well! No wonder the dogs don't bark at him," said Mother.

When Star's little friends came home from kindergarten, Star was swinging on the gate. "Hello, Lillybell!" she called out. "We have a new mailman and he carries candy in his pockets—candy for the dogs in one pocket and candy for the children in the other pocket."

"Did he give you some?" asked Lillybell.

"Uh-huh," said Star. "He gave some to Butch too."

A little later Rickie appeared. "Hello, Rickie!" Star called. "We have a new mailman. He gives candy to all the dogs and they don't bark at him. And he gives candy to the children too."

"Would he give some to me?" Rickie asked.

"If you were home, he would," said Star. "But you're in kindergarten when he comes."

A little later Polly and Rosemary came by. When they saw Star, they stopped.

"We have a new mailman," said Star. "He carries candy in his pockets for the dogs and he gives me candy too."

"I don't believe it," said Rosemary.

"It's true," said Star.

"No, it isn't," said Polly. "You're just making it up."

"It is so true," said Star. "Just you wait until Saturday."

The following morning Star was downstairs very early. When Betsy left for school, Star said, "Mother, what time is it?"

"It's half past eight," said Mother.

"Will you tell me when it's quarter past nine, Mother?" said Star.

"I'll try to remember," said her mother.

At quarter to nine Star said, "Is it quarter past nine yet?"

"Not yet," said Mother.

At nine o'clock Star said, "Is it quarter past nine yet?"

"Not yet," answered Mother. "Where ever are you going at quarter past nine?"

"I'm going to ride my tricycle over to Butch's house," Star replied.

"I see," said Mother.

At twenty minutes past nine Star rode up to Butch's house on her tricycle.

"Hello!" she called to Butch, who was lifting his tricycle down the front steps. "Has the mailman come yet?"

"Not yet," said Butch.

Star and Butch rode up and down on the pavement and watched for the mailman. Joey ran beside them. Pretty soon they heard him whistling. They rode up the street toward the sound and met the mailman at the corner.

"Hi!" cried Butch.

"Hello!" cried Star.

"Hello!" said the mailman.

"Have you got some candy for Joey?" Butch asked.

The mailman put his hand in his pocket and pulled out a piece of candy. He gave it to Joey. Then he put his hand in his other pocket and took out two pieces of candy. He gave one to Star and one to Butch.

The children said, "Thank you."

As the mailman walked away, Star and Butch unwrapped their pieces of candy. Then they popped them into their mouths and rode

off in the opposite direction from the mail-man. They rode around the block until they reached Star's house. There they rode up and down and watched for the mailman again.

After a while they heard him whistling. Star and Butch set off at full speed toward the corner with Thumpy running close be-hind. There they met the mailman again.

"Hi!" cried Butch.

"Hello!" cried Star.

"Why, hello!" said the mailman.

"Have you got a piece of candy for Thumpy?" Star asked.

"Certainly have," said the mailman, reach-ing into his pocket.

Star and Butch watched to see if the mail-man was going to put his hand in his other pocket, but he didn't. Instead, he went up to the house where the brown cocker spaniel lived and dropped the mail through the slot.

Star and Butch waited for him. Then, one on each side of him, they rode along to the next gate.

Butch looked up at the mailman and said, "Did you give candy to very many dogs this morning?"

"A good many," replied the mailman.

"And did you give candy to many children?" asked Star.

"Oh, I gave some to two children I met on the corner of Oak Road," said the mailman. "They were riding tricycles."

"What did they look like?" Butch asked.

"Well, one was a little girl with pigtails that looked like paintbrushes, and the other was a boy with red hair."

"Were they us?" asked Star.

"Come to think of it, they looked a good bit like you, but I guess they couldn't have been, because they were riding on Oak Road," said the mailman. And he put his hand in his left pocket and pulled out two pieces of candy.

Star and Butch said, "Thank you."

As Star tore the paper off her piece of candy, she said, "It *was* us." And then the mailman and Star and Butch all laughed very hard.

The following day was Saturday. Early in the morning all of Star's friends from the kindergarten were out watching for the mailman.

At quarter past nine Star set off on her tricycle for Butch's house. She met Rickie before she reached the corner. "I'm going to Butch's house to meet the mailman," she said.

Rickie ran beside Star and soon they came upon Lillybell. "We're going to meet the mailman," said Rickie. Lillybell ran along with Rickie and Star.

Then they met Rosemary and Polly. They, too, were waiting for the mailman.

By the time the mailman arrived at Butch's house, there were ten children waiting with Star and Butch. When he saw them he cried out, "Jumping catfish! Who are these?"

"They're from kindergarten," said Star.

"We told them about the candy," said Butch.

"I thought so," said the mailman as he handed the candy from his left pocket to the outstretched hands.

The mailman moved on to deliver the mail while the children unwrapped the candy.

"Now," said Butch, with his mouth full, "we'll all go over to Star's house."

The flock of children, led by Star and Butch, trooped around the block. In a few minutes

twelve children were hanging over the white picket fence in front of Star's house. They were waiting for the mailman.

At last they heard him whistling. They saw him turn the corner and go up to the front door of the house where the brown cocker spaniel lived. They watched him as he closed the gate. Then to their great surprise he crossed the street and went out of sight beyond the corner house.

The children waited a long time. Then they ran to the corner and looked up the street, but there was no mailman in sight.

One by one the children were called home for their lunch.

After Star had had her lunch, she went into the front hall. There, lying on the rug under the slot in the door, were some letters.

As Star picked them up she said, "Now, when do you suppose that mailman left these letters!"

On Monday morning Star was swinging on the front gate when Lillybell went past on her way to kindergarten. Lillybell's mother was with her and Lillybell was crying. "I don't want to go to kindergarten!" she wailed. "I don't want to go to kindergarten! I want to wait for the mailman."

After a while Star looked down the street and there she saw Rickie hanging on to the fence rails, while his big brother tugged at his other hand. "I don't want to go to kindergarten!" cried Rickie. "I want to wait for the mailman."

All over the neighborhood the children were crying, "I don't want to go to kindergarten. I want to wait for the mailman."

At quarter past nine Star climbed on her tricycle. She called to her mother, "Goodbye, Mother! I'm going over to Butch's to meet the mailman. But I'll be back soon."

CHAPTER VIII

The Santa Claus Parade

It was the middle of November, but the days were still sunshiny and the sun was still warm. It was hard to believe that it would soon be Thanksgiving.

Star's little friends were looking forward to Thanksgiving Day, not just because there would be turkey but because there would be a parade—the Santa Claus Parade.

Every year the big stores in the town had a parade. So on Thanksgiving morning all the children stood on the sidewalk and watched for Santa Claus to pass by. But this year many of the children were to be in the parade.

One day Rickie came to play with Star after school.

"The kindergarten is going to be in the Santa Claus Parade on Thanksgiving Day," said Rickie.

"You mean you're going to walk in the street?" asked Star.

"Oh, no!" said Rickie. "We're going to be on a float."

"How can you float in a parade?" said Star. "You have to have water to float. Like I floated in the ocean last summer."

"This is going to be the Old Woman Who Lived in a Shoe float," said Rickie.

"But where is the shoe going to float?" said Star.

"It isn't going to float," said Rickie. "It's a float."

"But where is the water?" asked Star.

"There isn't any water," shouted Rickie. "I told you it isn't going to float."

"You said it was going to float," said Star.

"I did not," yelled Rickie. "I said it was going to *be* a float."

"Well, there isn't any water," said Star. "So it can't float without water."

"It's a float. It's a float," shouted Rickie.

"It is not," shouted Star. "There isn't any water."

"What are you two quarreling about?" asked Betsy, who had just come home from school.

"Rickie says he's going to be in the Santa Claus Parade. He says the Old Woman Who Lived in a Shoe is going to float, and there isn't any water for her shoe to float in, is there, Betsy?"

"Oh," said Betsy, "this is a different kind of a float, Star. The float that Rickie means is a great big platform on a truck. The Old Woman Who Lived in a Shoe will ride on the platform with all her children around her on the float."

"See!" said Rickie. "Didn't I tell you?"

"I'm going to be on a float too," said Betsy.

"What are you going to be?" Star asked.

"I'm going to be on the Mother Goose float. I'm going to be Mary, Mary, Quite Contrary. I'm going to carry a watering can. And Billy Porter is going to be Little Jack Horner."

"Who's going to be Mother Goose?" asked Star.

"Nobody," said Betsy. "Mother Goose is going to be a great big goose made out of something. Paper, I guess. Or maybe cloth."

"What's Eddie Wilson going to be?" Star asked.

"Oh, Eddie's going to be on one of the fairy-tale floats," said Betsy. "He's going to be Jack and the Beanstalk and Ellen is going to be Goldilocks."

"What am I going to be?" Star asked.

"Oh, you can't be in the parade," said Betsy. "You're too little."

"If you were in kindergarten, you could be one of the children that lived in the shoe," said Rickie.

Star's lower lip began to tremble. "I want to be in the parade," she said.

Just then Star's father came in. "Father!" cried Star. "I want to be in the parade. Betsy is going to be Mary, Mary, Quite Contrary, and Rickie is going to be an Old Woman in the Shoe's little boy, and they're going to float. Only not in the water. I want to float too."

"Oh, Star! You and I are going to watch the

parade," said Father. "If everyone was in the parade there wouldn't be anyone to watch it."

This made Star feel a little better, but not much.

When Thanksgiving morning came, everyone woke up to find that the sun was not shining and it was a very cold day. The sky was gray and the wind was blowing.

"Betsy," said her mother, "you'll have to wear your winter coat in the parade. You'll freeze if you don't."

"Oh, Mother!" cried Betsy. "How can I wear a coat? No one can see my old-fashioned dress with the hoop skirt if I wear a coat. I can wear two sweaters under my dress. They'll keep me warm."

"But your legs will be cold," said Mother. "If you wear sweaters instead of a coat, you'll have to wear your snow pants."

"Snow pants!" cried Betsy. "My pantalets with the ruffles have to show below my dress. What will I look like with snow pants showing? Who ever heard of anyone wearing snow pants when they're carrying a watering can? I'd have to carry a muff with snow pants."

"Now, don't make such a fuss. Your ruffles will show," said Mother.

Mother took Betsy's snow pants out of the closet and carried them away. Betsy began putting on her sweaters.

A short time later Mother returned with Betsy's snow pants. On each leg she had sewn three rows of white ruffles. "There are your pantalets with the ruffles," she said.

Betsy took them from Mother. She held them up, laughing. "Oh, Mother!" she cried. "You're wonderful! No one will ever know they are snow pants."

Mother took a woolen cap out of the drawer and handed it to Betsy.

"But, Mother, I have to wear a sunbonnet!"

"Put the cap on first," said Mother, "and put the sunbonnet over it."

Betsy did as she was told. The sunbonnet hid the woolen cap. Betsy laughed. "Now I guess you'll want me to wear mittens."

"Of course you must wear mittens," said Mother, pulling open another drawer.

"Mother, I can't wear mittens. Who ever heard of anyone wearing mittens when they were carrying a watering can?"

"You must wear mittens," said Mother, "or your hands will freeze."

Mother took a pair of pale pink woolen mittens from the drawer and handed them to Betsy. "No one will know you're wearing mittens," she said. "These will look like your hands."

Betsy laughed again as she pulled on the mittens.

Betsy was dressed now, and when she looked at herself in the long mirror, she just looked like a very fat Mary, Mary, Quite Contrary. No one would have known that she was all bundled up in winter woolens.

"What am I going to wear?" asked Star.

"You're going to wear your new brown snowsuit," said Mother. "I'm glad I don't have to dress you up to look like a nursery rhyme or a fairy tale."

"But I would like to look like a nursery rhyme or a fairy tale," said Star. "Then I could be in the parade."

Mother helped Star into her snow pants and buttoned her little brown jacket. When Star put on her brown pointed hood, Father said, "Well, you look just like a little brownie."

"She looks like one of the Seven Little Dwarfs," said Betsy.

When Star heard this, she ran off to the playroom and came back with the gray beard that she had worn on Halloween. "I'm going to wear this and make believe I'm a dwarf," she said.

"Very well," said Father, "but come along. We have to take Betsy over to the school, where they are making up the floats."

Star and Betsy climbed into the car beside their father and off they went.

When they reached the school, there were a great many boys and girls in the school yard. A very fat Jack and the Beanstalk was chasing a rolypoly Little Boy Blue. Little Jack Horner had so many clothes on that his coat had been slit up the back and fastened to a warm jacket underneath with big safety pins. But they would not show when he sat in his corner.

Little Red Riding Hood looked like a big rubber ball, and Jack and Jill were wearing so many clothes, they could hardly waddle.

Lined up by the curb were ten coal trucks, each with a big platform fastened on top of it. Big letters on the sides of the trucks told

what each float was. Betsy was lifted up on
the one that said MOTHER GOOSE.

The Seven Dwarfs, looking like fat brown
chestnuts, were being lifted up on their float.
Star and her father were standing beside the
driver's seat. One by one the little dwarfs
were lifted up by the driver. Up they went—
one, two, three, four, five, six, seven.

After the driver had lifted the seventh little dwarf up on the float, he looked at Star.
"Oh! Here's another one," he said. And he
picked up Star and placed her on the float
with the other dwarfs.

Star's eyes were big with surprise as she
looked down at Father. Father was laughing.

As the float moved off, Father waved his hand and called, "Have a good time, Star. You're in the parade after all."

Star waved back and called, "I'm floating, Father. I'm floating."

And that is how it happened that there were eight little dwarfs instead of seven little dwarfs in the Santa Claus Parade.

CHAPTER IX

The Present That Had No Shape

Christmas was coming and Star's birthday was coming too. Star had been born on Christmas Eve, so her birthday was the twenty-fourth of December. This meant that Star had presents on two days. Father said he was sure that Santa Claus always fell over Star's birthday presents when he brought her Christmas presents into the house.

One evening Star was sitting on her father's lap. A fire burned in the fireplace and

Star felt very cozy. She snuggled down in her father's arms.

"Tell me, Twinkle," said Father. "What do you want for Christmas?"

"First you have to ask me what I want for my birthday," said Star. " 'Cause my birthday comes first."

"So it does!" said Father. "We'll begin over again. What would you like to have for your birthday?"

"First you guess. See if you can guess," said Star, resting her head against her father's shoulder.

Father began to guess. "A new painting book?" he asked.

"Yes," said Star. "A new painting book."

"I'm a good guesser," said Father.

"Guess again," said Star.

"A catalooper?" said Father.

Star sat up and looked at her father in surprise. "A what?" she asked.

"I said a catalooper," said Father.

"I never heard of a catalooper," said Star.

"I've never heard of one either," said Father. And Father and Star both laughed.

"Now, Father," said Star, "guess some more."

"Oh, my!" said Father. "This is going to be hard. You'll have to help me. What shape is it? Is it round?"

"No, it isn't round," said Star.

"Is it square?" Father asked.

"No." Star laughed. "It isn't square."

"Is it long?" said Father.

Star was laughing harder now. "No, no!" she cried. "It isn't long."

"Then it must be short," said Father.

"No, no, no!" Star shouted with laughter.

"Oh, dear!" said Father. "Help me a little bit. Just a little."

Star doubled over on her father's lap, laughing. When she could stop laughing she said, "It hasn't any shape at all!"

"What! No shape?" cried Father. "A present without a shape, Twinkle?"

Star nodded her head. "That's right."

Father wrinkled his forehead and made his face look very long. "Oh, Twinkle!" he said. "I can't think of a present without a shape. Toys have shapes. Dolls have shapes. Animals have shapes. Books have shapes. How can I wrap it up in paper and tie it with ribbon if it doesn't have any shape?"

Star buried her face in her father's neck and laughed and laughed. "Oh, Father," she cried, "you can't wrap the present that I want in paper. You can't tie it with ribbon."

"Then I give up," said Father. "You'll have to tell me what it is you want for a birthday present."

"I want to go to kindergarten," Star shouted. "That's what I want for my birthday. I told you it didn't have any shape."

"It certainly doesn't." Father laughed.

"Do you think I'll get the present?" Star asked.

"I don't know, Twinkle," said Father, "but we shall see."

"I'll be five years old," said Star. "I'll be old enough to go to kindergarten."

"I know that," said Father, "but I don't believe they'll take you in on the very day you are five. I think you'll have to wait until the new term begins."

"But they said I could come when I was five," said Star.

"Well, we shall see," said Father.

On the morning of December twenty-fourth Star woke up feeling that something exciting was going to happen. She lay very still and made believe she was not awake. She was trying to remember what day it was. Could it be Christmas? Star peeked out over the covers and looked at the footboard of her bed. No, it couldn't be Christmas, thought Star. It couldn't be Christmas, because her stocking wasn't hanging on the footboard.

Just then Betsy poked her head in the door and called out, "Happy Birthday, Twinkle!"

Betsy handed her a package tied up with red ribbon. Star sat up in bed and untied the ribbon and unwrapped the box. She lifted the lid, and there were the red shoes she had wanted.

"Oh, thank you!" Star cried. "They're beautiful!"

Star jumped out of bed and put on the new red shoes. Then she put on her blue woolly bathrobe and went downstairs to find her mother.

"Look, Mother," she said. "I have on my new red shoes."

"Good morning, darling," said Mother. "Happy Birthday!"

Mother kissed her five times. Then she said, "Hurry up and dress. We're going over to school with Betsy for the Christmas concert."

Star went upstairs. She washed her face and cleaned her teeth. She put on her peppermint-stick dress. Betsy came in to braid her hair and tie her red ribbons.

"I like my red shoes," said Star, looking down at her feet.

"You must keep them to wear when you go to kindergarten," said Betsy.

"I'm five now," said Star. "Will I go to kindergarten right away?"

"I don't know," said Betsy.

At Star's place at the breakfast table there was a new painting book and a little gold bracelet. Star was delighted with her presents.

As soon as Star and Betsy had finished their breakfast, Mother hustled them into the car.

When they reached the school, Betsy went to her classroom, and Star and her mother went into the assembly room. It was a big room with rows and rows of seats. In the front of the room there was a stage with a green velvet curtain. In the back of the room there were extra chairs for the parents of the children. Billy Porter's mother and Mrs. Wilson were there. Star's mother sat down beside Mrs. Porter. Star sat on a chair beside her mother. All Star could see was the back of the chair in front of her.

"Mother," said Star, "I can't see anything."

"You can sit on my lap when the concert begins," said Mother.

Star sat still. Her legs stuck out straight in front of her. She looked at her new red shoes and thought how pretty they were.

More and more mothers came to sit on the chairs in the back of the room. There were a few fathers too.

Suddenly there was music. Someone was playing the piano. Star couldn't see anything,

but she could hear the tramp, tramp of feet. The children were marching into the assembly room. Star climbed up and stood on her seat. She could see all over the room now. She saw her little kindergarten friends marching into the room. There was Rosemary at the head of the line. She could see Rickie and Lillybell and Polly. She could see all her friends.

When all the children were seated, Mother took Star on her lap. Just then Miss Morse stood up in the front of the room. She looked at the back of the room and said, "I see little Star back there. We would like her to walk up here and sit with the kindergarten."

Star got down off her mother's lap. It was a long walk up the aisle to where the kindergarten children were sitting. Star felt much too happy to walk. She skipped all the way. She skipped all the way in her new red shoes.

When all was quiet, Betsy walked up to the platform and read the Twenty-third Psalm— "The Lord is my shepherd."

Then Miss Morse said that the kindergarten would sing.

The kindergarten children stood up. They marched up on the stage and stood in a line.

Star went with them and stood between Rickie and Lillybell. When they sang their song, Star sang, too, for it was the song she had learned when she sat inside of the little house in the kindergarten room.

When the children had taken their seats again, the green velvet curtain was lifted and the concert began. Star loved the concert.

First of all there was the song of the Christmas fairies. Twelve little girls, dressed as fairies, sang the song.

Then there was the song of Santa Claus and his helpers. Rudy Wilson was Santa Claus. He wore a red suit stuffed with pillows to make him look fat. Billy Porter, the Wilson twins, and three other boys were Santa Claus's helpers. They wore red suits, too, but they were not as fat as Santa Claus and their beards were not as long. They all shook sleigh bells as they sang.

Star liked the song of the Christmas cookies best. Seven children dressed to look like big Christmas cookies sang:

"We are the Christmas cookies
Baked in the oven for you."

Everyone laughed when they heard this and they laughed at Eddie Wilson too. Eddie was right in the middle of the seven children. He was dressed like a gingerbread boy.

When the concert was over, Miss Morse told Star to go back to her mother. Star was sorry, because she thought she was going to stay with her little friends and go into the kindergarten room. Star didn't skip as she went back to her mother. She walked very slowly.

After all the children had returned to their classrooms and the parents had said good-bye to each other, Mother and Star walked toward the big front door of the school. But instead of going out of the door, Mother led Star to the door of the kindergarten. Mother opened the door and Star walked in. As she did so, the kindergarten children all began to sing:

> "*Happy Birthday to you,*
> *Happy Birthday to you,*
> *Happy Birthday, dear Twinkle,*
> *Happy Birthday to you.*"

The children were standing in their places around the big kindergarten table. Miss Morse led Star to the end of the table. There on the table was a birthday cake with five red candles.

Star's eyes were as bright as the candles. Now she knew that this was a birthday party. It was her birthday party.

Miss Morse held Star's little pigtails while she leaned over and blew out the candles. Then Miss Morse helped her to cut the cake, and Mother put a plate of ice cream in front of each of the children.

That evening when Star saw her father, she cried, "Father! Guess what! Guess what, Father!"

"I can guess," said Father. "You went to kindergarten!"

"Yes, I did!" said Star. "I was invited. And

I sang. And they had a birthday party for me."

Then Star's face grew sober. She sighed a deep sigh. "Oh, Father!" she said. "Do you think they will let me go to kindergarten every day, now that I'm five years old?"

Father lifted Star up on his knee. "I'm going to tell you a story," he said.

Star snuggled into his arms.

"Once upon a time," said Father, "there was a little girl who wanted to go to kindergarten."

"It was me, wasn't it?" said Star.

Father looked at his little girl and said, "Well, come to think of it, she looked like you."

Star settled back against her father's shoulder.

Father went on with his story. "Well, this little girl wished that she could go to kindergarten. She wished and she wished. She used to swing on the garden gate and watch her friends go by on their way to kindergarten. But she couldn't go because she was only four years old. But at last the day came when she was five years old. It was the day before Christmas. Of course, she couldn't go to kindergarten on Christmas Day and she couldn't go to kindergarten during the holidays, but when school opened again, the little girl didn't have to swing on the gate and watch her friends go by. No, indeed! She went with them to kindergarten, for now she was five years old."

"Oh, Father!" said Star. "It's my present, isn't it?"

"Yes," said Father. "The present that has no shape."

CHAPTER X

Lillybell Didn't Forget

On the third day of January Star was up before anyone in the house. This was the day she had waited for. This was the day she was going to school with her little friends. She looked out of the window. It had snowed during the night but now it had stopped. Star was glad it had stopped snowing, because she wanted to walk to school. She wanted to walk with Lillybell and Rickie and Rosemary and Polly.

123

By the time Mother was up Star was all dressed.

"Goodness!" cried Mother. "You did get up early, Twinkle."

"I'm going to kindergarten," said Star, putting on her brown hood.

"Not before breakfast, darling," said Mother.

"I don't want to be late," said Star.

"You won't be late," replied Mother. "Betsy isn't out of bed yet."

"She'll be late," said Star, pulling on her snow pants.

"Twinkle, you'll be baked in those snow pants," said Mother. "You don't have to leave for over an hour."

"Lillybell might come for me early," said Star, taking her coat off its hanger.

"Now, Star! Don't put your coat on," said Mother. "You'll be too warm."

"All right," said Star, "but I'll take it downstairs."

Star followed her mother downstairs. She laid her coat on a chair beside the front door. Then she went into the kitchen. "Is breakfast almost ready, Mother?" she asked.

"Good gracious!" her mother cried. "I just came into the kitchen. Give me a little time."

Star ran to the front door and looked up the street. "I don't see Lillybell," she said when she returned to the kitchen. "Shall I sit up at the table, Mother?"

"Yes," said her mother. "Sit up at the table and drink your orange juice."

Star climbed up on her chair and drank her orange juice. When she finished, she got down and ran upstairs. Mother had just put a dish of cereal at her place when she returned.

"I had to get my mittens," said Star, out of breath.

When she finished her cereal, she climbed the stairs again. Mother was putting a soft-boiled egg at her place. "Now what?" said Mother.

"I had to get Koala Bear," said Star. "I think he would like to go to kindergarten."

Just as Star was about to climb up on her chair, she changed her mind and ran to the front window. When she came back, she said, "You don't think Lillybell will forget to stop for me, do you?"

"Lillybell will come for you, I'm sure," said her mother. "Now, don't get off that chair until you have finished your breakfast."

Star began to eat her egg and toast. In a few

minutes she heard Father coming downstairs. "Father!" she called. "Will you open the front door, please, and find out for me if Lillybell is coming?"

Father opened the front door and looked outside. When he came into the dining room, he said, "I don't see her."

"You don't think that Lillybell forgot, do you, Mother?" Star asked.

"Lillybell will be here," said her mother.

Star stood looking out of the window while Father and Betsy ate their breakfast. At last she saw Lillybell coming down the street. Behind Lillybell she could see Rickie.

Star rushed to get her coat. "Here comes Lillybell!" she cried. "Here comes Lillybell! And Rickie too!"

Star scrambled into her coat and pulled on her mittens. Then she couldn't fasten her galoshes, because the mittens made her fingers so thick. "I can't fasten my galoshes!" she cried. "Father, I can't fasten my galoshes."

Father came to help Star. He sat her up on the chair and fastened her galoshes.

There was a knock at the door. "Come in, Lillybell," Star called. Then she called to her mother, "Open the door, Mother. Please open the door for Lillybell."

Mother came and opened the door for Lillybell

"Is Star ready to go to kindergarten?" Lillybell asked.

"I'm ready!" Star called out. "I'm all ready."

Just as the two children were going out of the door, Mother said, "Star! Is your hair combed?"

"Oh," said Star, "it was combed yesterday."

Mother pulled her back into the house. "You can't go to kindergarten with your hair not combed," said Mother.

"Oh, dear!" cried Star. "I'll be late."

"No, you won't be late," said Mother as she pushed Star upstairs. "And Lillybell will wait for you."

Mother took off Star's hood and brushed and braided her hair. Then she tied the braids with red ribbons.

Meanwhile the crowd at the front door was growing. When Star was ready to leave, there were Lillybell and Rickie and Rosemary and Polly. Just as the children went out of the gate, Toni came along.

The six children scampered along, making

footprints in the snow. When they reached the corner they met Butch. Butch had his sled.

"Hello, Butch!" Star called out. "I'm going to kindergarten."

Butch watched Star and the children as they turned the corner.

When the mailman came, he found Butch sitting on his sled. Joey and Thumpy were sitting beside him.

"Hello!" said the mailman. "Where's your friend Twinkle?"

"She's gone to kindergarten," said Butch, "but I'll save her piece of candy for her if you want me to."